Silver Dolphins

THE MAGIC CHARM

For Antonia MacPhee - My Dolphin Girl

First published in paperback by HarperCollins *Children's Books* in 2009

HarperCollins *Children's Books* is a division of HarperCollins *Publishers* Ltd,
77-85 Fulham Palace Road, Hammersmith, London W6 8JB.

Visit our website at: www.harpercollins.co.uk

1 3 5 7 9 10 8 6 4 2
ISBN-13: 978-0-00-730968-9

A CIP catalogue record for this title is available from the British Library.

by Summer Waters

Silver Dolphins

THE MAGIC CHARM

HarperCollins *Children's Books*

Prologue

Out at sea thirty dolphins waited anxiously for their leader to arrive. Some of them whispered together in low whistles and clicks. Others stayed silent, scanning the horizon with bright eyes. One little dolphin couldn't keep still. He rolled in the water, butting his sister with his silver head, calling for her to play with him.

"Mum," squeaked Dream crossly. "Bubbles is annoying me."

"Hush now," their mother clicked back. "Your father's coming."

Bubbles stopped teasing his big sister.

"I see him," he whistled, his tail smacking the

water excitedly. "Can I go and meet him, Mum?"

"No, darling. You must wait here with everyone else."

Bubbles bobbed in the water, clicking impatiently, until the large dolphin with a striking yellow blaze along his side drew nearer, then he too fell silent. Spirit, the large dolphin, halted a tail's length in front of the pod and slowly bowed his magnificent head.

"Our search is over," he announced. "At last we have found a new Silver Dolphin."

An excited whistle rippled from the pod through the water.

"Our new Silver Dolphin is young," Spirit continued. "She has much to learn, but she is a very special child and I know she will serve us well. Be kind to her. Help her to fulfil her tasks and in return she will help us."

"When will we meet her?" squeaked Bubbles, the words bursting from his mouth before he could stop them.

Spirit smiled.

"Soon," he whistled. "Very soon."

Chapter One

"What are Lauren and Becky doing?"

Antonia Lee and her best friend Sophie Hastings were walking across the school field of Sandy Bay Primary after a game of rounders when Antonia suddenly changed direction.

"Oh, that's mean! They're teasing a frog." Antonia broke into a run shouting, "Leave it alone. That's cruel."

Lauren laughed and continued poking the frog with her rounders bat, cheering each time the frog jumped forward.

Angrily Antonia squatted down and scooped the frog into her hands.

"That's Lauren's frog," said Becky, stepping towards her. "She's teaching it to jump."

"You're cruel," said Antonia hotly. "How would you like to be poked with a rounders bat?"

"Eeewww, that's gross! She's touching it." Lauren backed away. "Come on, Becky. Game over."

Antonia cradled the frog in her hands. Its lumpy brown body quivered with fright and its eyes bulged with uncertainty.

"I'm going to put him in the school pond," she told Sophie. "Will you come with me?"

Sophie sighed. "You like all animals, don't you, even the ugly ones?"

"Not all animals," Antonia grinned cheekily. "People are animals too, but I don't like Lauren and Becky."

"Becky's all right when you get to know her," said Sophie unexpectedly. "She comes to one of Dad's art classes."

Sophie's father was an artist who ran classes from his studio. When she wasn't busy daydreaming Sophie helped him out, setting up easels and handing round paintbrushes.

"Please will you come to the pond with me?" Antonia changed the subject, not wanting to argue.

"Of course I'll come."

"We'll have to be quick. We've got afternoon assembly next because a visitor's coming in to tell us who won the poster competition."

Carefully Antonia carried the frog to the pond and left it on the water's edge in the shade of some reeds. When she and Sophie returned to class, 5B were changing out of their PE kits and back into school uniform. Miss Brown frowned.

"Where have you two been? Don't tell me, you stopped to have a chat. Hurry up, girls, or you'll make us all late."

Antonia changed quickly, trying not to be the last to line up at the door. When everyone was ready Miss Brown led the class along to the hall. As Antonia filed in, she stared curiously at the woman sitting next to their head teacher. The visitor had a faraway look on her face as if she was thinking about something special.

"She looks like a sea witch," whispered Sophie dramatically. "Oh, poo! There's no room to sit together."

The visitor had wild brown hair and seaweed-green clothes, but Antonia thought her face was too kind to belong to a witch. She stifled a giggle as Sophie, pulling faces, reluctantly started a new line. When the whole school was assembled the woman stood up, smiling broadly so that her green eyes disappeared into her wrinkled face.

"Good afternoon, children. My name is Claudia Neal and I'm responsible for arranging the poster competition you've all entered. The competition was held to launch Sea Watch. It's a local charity involved in marine conservation and animal rescue, and I'm hoping that some of you might volunteer to help with it. There are many things to do at Sea Watch and lots of injured birds and animals to look after. I'd be thrilled if some of you could come along. But right now I'm going to tell you the winners of the competition."

An excited buzz filled the hall. Antonia grinned across at Sophie, sitting a whole line away from

her. She was sure Sophie had won. She was a fantastic artist and had painted an amazing picture of dolphins leaping in the bay. Antonia had drawn dolphins too, but her picture didn't look anywhere near as good as Sophie's. Especially after she'd covered it with facts about pollution and how harmful it was to sea life.

"The standard of entries was very high and there are two runners-up: Joe Piper in 3T and Eleanor Jacobs in 6D."

Antonia clapped loudly as Joe and Eleanor made their way to the front of the hall to collect their prizes – illustrated books about the sea – but all the time her eyes were on Sophie. She had to be the winner. She just had to be.

"And the winner, chosen not just for her super picture of dolphins, but for all the interesting facts she included as well, is Antonia Lee in 5B."

At first Antonia didn't register that she'd won. She was too busy staring at Sophie, who looked like she'd been knocked over the head with a bucket full of fish. Antonia tried to catch her friend's eye, but Sophie didn't look in her direction.

"Go on. Get your prize."

The boy sitting next to Antonia practically pushed her to her feet. Self-consciously Antonia stumbled through the rows of seated children to the front of the hall where Claudia was waiting.

"Well done, my dear," she said, grasping Antonia's hand. "You obviously care about dolphins and the sea."

"I do," said Antonia, her grey-green eyes shining eagerly. "I can see the sea from my bedroom window. There's a pod of common dolphins that swim in the bay early in the evening. I love watching them."

"I've seen them too." Claudia gripped Antonia's hand and stared into her eyes.

Antonia caught her breath. Claudia's gaze was so intense that for a second it felt like she was tapping into her thoughts. Maybe she *was* a witch! Then Claudia smiled and letting go of Antonia's hand she gave her a small box. Antonia opened it and gasped. Inside was a silver dolphin on a delicate chain.

"It's beautiful."

Claudia smiled and said so softly that Antonia struggled to hear her, "Always answer the dolphin's call."

"What...?"

Questions lined up at Antonia's lips, but before she could ask anything Claudia returned to her seat. Mr Cordier, the head teacher, waved Antonia back to her place.

"Well done, everyone," he said. "And if any of

you are interested in marine conservation, remember that Sea Watch needs volunteers. See me after assembly if you'd like more details."

Antonia sat down. Had Claudia really just said 'answer the dolphin's call'? What could that mean? Antonia stared at Claudia, but she was gazing out of the window as if she'd rather be somewhere else. Antonia decided to ask her mum if she could volunteer. Helping out at Sea Watch sounded like great fun.

Antonia looked at the necklace again. She ran her finger over the dolphin charm. To her surprise the metal was smooth and slippery, just how she imagined a real dolphin would feel. She couldn't wait to wear it and show Sophie, but she had the strangest feeling that she shouldn't put it on until she was alone. Assembly seemed to go on for ever, but at last it was over and everyone went back to their classrooms. It was home time and there was the usual scramble to stack chairs and collect bags and lunchboxes. Several girls crowded round Antonia wanting to see her prize. Antonia was showing them when she noticed Sophie was missing. She looked around and spotted her friend heading out of the classroom door.

"Sophie, wait."

Antonia closed the box and ran after Sophie, catching her up in the corridor.

"Going without me?" she joked.

Sophie rolled her eyes. "Hurry up then. You know I help Dad with his four o'clock art class."

"Sorry, I forgot. Everyone wanted to see my prize. It's a dolphin necklace. Look!" Excitedly Antonia thrust the box at Sophie.

"Nice," said Sophie, barely glancing at it.

"Nice?" echoed Antonia. "Is that it?"

"I've told you. I'm in a hurry," Sophie snapped.

"There's plenty of time. Do you want to try my necklace on?"

Antonia held her breath, suddenly hoping Sophie would refuse. The two girls usually shared everything, but somehow Antonia was reluctant to share her necklace. It was too special.

"No, thanks," said Sophie. "Shame you didn't win something bigger, like a trophy. That looks a bit, you know, throwaway."

"Hey!"

Antonia's cheeks flushed. She didn't care that her necklace was small; it was still special.

"Aren't you pleased for me? You've got hundreds of trophies for art, but this is the first time I've won anything."

"Well done," said Sophie, walking faster. "I'm very pleased for you. But your picture wasn't art.

If it had been... Oh, never mind. Are you coming with me or waiting for your mum?"

Antonia stared at her friend. She thought Sophie would be as excited by her win as she was, but she sounded almost cross about it. Was it because she was surprised that Antonia had won instead of her?

"Well?" asked Sophie impatiently.

Antonia hesitated.

Mrs Lee worked in the office at Sandy Bay Primary School. Antonia usually walked home with her friend. But she was dying to tell her mum she'd won the competition, still, she didn't want to fall out with Sophie.

"Look, I'm sorry. I didn't mean to be snappy. The necklace is lovely." Sophie smiled. "I'll try it on when I'm not in such a rush. Now are you coming with me or not?"

Relieved, Antonia smiled back. "Of course," she said, tucking the necklace box in her bag. "What are you waiting for?"

A short while later the girls arrived at Sophie's house.

"Do you want to come round tomorrow?" asked Sophie, stopping on the drive. "If it's hot we could go down to the beach."

"What time? I've got my surfing class in the morning."

"After lunch. Dad'll have finished his classes by then so he can take us. Say about half one?"

The girls always made sure an adult was with them when they went swimming – Antonia's parents were quite strict about it.

"Half one's fine," agreed Antonia. "See you tomorrow." She walked to the end of Sophie's road in the direction of home, but then stopped. She couldn't wait a second longer. Now she was on her own she had to try on her dolphin necklace. Antonia shrugged her school bag from her shoulders and, pulling out the box, opened it. Sunlight flashed on the dolphin charm and the dolphin's silver eye seemed to wink at her. Antonia ran a finger along its streamlined body, wondering again at how life-like it felt. With trembling fingers she lifted the necklace from its bed of silk and pushing her long blonde hair out of the way she fastened it around her neck. The dolphin felt strange against her skin, soft and slippery. Suddenly Antonia had a strong urge to be near the sea. At first she ignored it. She was supposed to go straight home, but as she walked the feeling grew too strong to be ignored. Antonia checked her watch. It was half past three, nearly half an hour before Mum and her little sister Jessica were due home. What harm could a quick diversion to the beach do?

Quickly, before she could change her mind, Antonia turned away from her own road and walked down the alley that led to the coastal path.

Chapter Two

Breaking into a jog Antonia followed the coastal path until it forked. Then turning right she scrambled down the tiny lane that led to Gull Bay, a secluded cove away from the main beach. The cove was empty. Antonia dumped her bag by a rock, pulled off her shoes and socks and ran across the powder-white sand to the sea.

"Oh!" she exclaimed, squinting into the afternoon sun. "Dolphins."

Four common dolphins, two large and two small, were swimming at the mouth of the cove. Excitedly Antonia waded into the water. She'd never seen them so close to the beach before. The largest dolphin had a distinctive yellow blaze that stretched from his face all the way to his dorsal fin. Awestruck, Antonia stared until a soft clicking noise caught her attention. It sounded like a dolphin, but it was too close to be coming from the dolphins in the sea. Something was tickling Antonia's neck. Her hand moved to her dolphin charm, soft and slippery against her skin. It was vibrating.

"What's happening?" whispered Antonia.

With a shaking hand she covered the dolphin necklace and the clicking noises softened. Thinking

she was imagining things Antonia uncovered the charm then quickly covered it again. The clicking grew loud then quiet like a radio being turned up and down. It can't be! Suddenly Antonia felt as if the dolphins were calling to her. They were telling her to swim out to them. But she wasn't allowed in the water alone. Mum and Dad had drummed that into her as soon as she was able to walk. The urge to swim to the dolphins was overwhelming. Antonia hitched her yellow checked school dress around her waist and splashed further into the sea. *This is wrong*, said her brain. *It's dangerous. You'll be grounded for ever if you get caught.* The water reached her chest. Antonia took a deep breath, stretched out her arms and swam.

Dangerous, dangerous, thrummed her brain.

It didn't feel dangerous. It felt like the most natural thing in the world. Antonia's legs seemed to meld together as they kicked out, dolphin-style. She was hardly aware of her clothes. Her body felt streamlined as it sliced through the waves of the incoming tide. It was exhilarating. As Antonia neared the dolphins she saw they were watching her and she hoped they wouldn't take fright and swim away. On impulse she called out, "Please stay."

Her voice, a shrill whistle, startled her. She cleared her throat and tried again but all that came out was a series of dolphin-like clicks. Antonia's brain whirled. What was happening to her? She cleared her throat.

"Hello," she spluttered, swallowing a mouthful of sea. "My name's Antonia."

There. She was speaking properly now. Maybe, for a second, the sea water had made her voice go funny. Then a strange clicking voice called out, "Silver Dolphin."

And with a whistle-like cry Antonia heard herself reply, "I'm coming."

She swam all the way up to the four dolphins and stopped in front of the largest. He stared at her, his eyes sparkling like sun on raindrops.

"Silver Dolphin," he clicked. "You answered the dolphin's call."

Antonia's head was dizzy with excitement. For ages she'd dreamt of swimming with the dolphins and now here she was, not just in the water with them, but talking to them too. How could that be? Was she turning into a dolphin? She glanced down at her legs and saw with relief that they were both still there.

The dolphin opened his mouth as if he were laughing at her.

"Believe it," he whistled kindly. "It's true. You are our new Silver Dolphin."

"Me? A Silver Dolphin? What does that mean?" she whistled back.

"It means that you will care for the sea and all the dolphins and creatures living here. It means that you will answer our call when we need help."

"That's what Claudia said I had to do when she gave me the necklace." Antonia stared at the dolphin. "Do you know Claudia?"

"Yes," the dolphin nodded. "And my name is Spirit. I'm the leader of a dolphin pod that lives out at sea. Pollution has been causing us terrible problems, but the Silver Dolphin makes things better for us. Sadly our Silver Dolphin can't swim with us now so you have been chosen for the role. Whenever pollution is causing harm we will call on you. If you don't want to help then you must say so now and we will search for a new Silver Dolphin."

Questions raced around Antonia's brain. Why had she been chosen to take the Silver Dolphin's place? Who had chosen her? And how did Claudia fit into all of this? There was so much she didn't understand. She wasn't even sure if this was really happening. Perhaps she'd fallen asleep and was having the most amazing dream. The four dolphins watched her expectantly.

"Please say yes," squeaked the littlest one.

Antonia stared at him. His eyes sparkled mischievously and he bobbed in the water as if he could hardly bear to keep still. He looked like Spirit, his silver body lined with a narrow stripe that ran from his eyes to his mouth and chin to flipper.

"Please?"

How could she refuse?

"Yes, I'd love to be your Silver Dolphin," she answered.

The dolphins stared blankly at her and Antonia realised she was speaking in her human voice. She tried again, concentrating hard on behaving like a dolphin and was overjoyed when her voice clicked out her reply. "Yes, I'll be your new Silver Dolphin."

"Bubbly!" The littlest dolphin squealed with excitement and swam in circles around Antonia.

"Bubbles, calm down," said Spirit sternly. "Bubbles is my youngest," he added. "Then there's Star, my wife, and Dream, my daughter."

Dream was only a bit larger than Bubbles, but seemed much more grown-up.

"Hello," she said indifferently.

Star was very pretty, with similar markings to Spirit only she was lighter in colour. She swam up to Antonia and gently rubbed her nose against Antonia's. "Thank you," she said. "It's not easy being a Silver Dolphin, but we will help you as much as we can."

"How will I know when I'm needed?" Antonia stuttered.

"You will hear our call," said Spirit.

Antonia touched her silver dolphin necklace.

"That's right," said Spirit. "The necklace is our link with you. I will call you again over the next few days so you can practise answering. Star is right. It's not easy being a Silver Dolphin. The work can be hard and dangerous."

Antonia's stomach fluttered. She desperately wanted to be a good Silver Dolphin, but would she be good enough?

"Can I teach her some swimming moves?" asked Bubbles. He leapt out of the water, his body making a perfect arch.

"Show off!" said Dream.

Spirit clicked a laugh.

"Not yet, Bubbles. Antonia needs time to take all this in. Let her go home now and we will call her again soon. Always wear your charm, Silver Dolphin. It is the only way we can call you."

Antonia didn't want to go back home. She wanted to swim with the dolphins, especially Bubbles, and learn all they could teach her. But she didn't dare disobey Spirit so she whistled a goodbye and headed back to the beach.

As she stepped out of the sea the water poured off her. By the time she'd padded back to her bag and shoes only her hair was slightly damp. Antonia clasped her hand over her dolphin charm. It was silent now, but its body still felt soft and slippery. Just like Star when she'd rubbed Antonia on the nose. Antonia grinned, then catching sight of her watch the grin immediately vanished.

"Oh, no!" she gasped.

It was nearly four o'clock. Her mum would be home any minute and if Antonia wasn't there she'd be in huge trouble. Shoving her feet in her shoes she snatched up her bag and raced up the beach.

Chapter Three

When Antonia arrived home she was surprised to find the house empty. For a guilty moment she wondered if Mum had gone out to look for her, but then the front door banged open and Mum and Jessica crowded into the tiny hall.

"Sorry, darling," Mum said, slipping out of her shoes and giving Antonia a hug. "We were late leaving school. Someone fell over in the playground and needed a plaster."

Antonia wriggled free.

"That's OK. Can I have something to eat?"

She was starving. *It must be all that swimming,* she thought, touching her dolphin charm.

"Yes, sure. What's that you're wearing?" replied Mum.

"It's a necklace. I won the Sea Watch competition."

"Did you? That's fantastic. Let's have a proper look."

Antonia swept back her long blonde hair so Mum could look at the necklace.

"It's beautiful."

"I know."

Antonia longed to say more. She wanted to tell her mother how the necklace had called her into the sea to swim with real dolphins. She was dying to say that she was the new Silver Dolphin. But she kept her mouth tightly shut. Mum would probably think she was mad. Besides, she had a feeling that the necklace might not work if she told people about it.

"Clever girl," said Mum proudly. "What did Sophie say? I bet she was pleased for you."

"I think so," said Antonia, remembering Sophie's comments and feeling slightly uncomfortable.

"No doubt she was surprised. It was a poster competition for the Sea Watch charity, wasn't it? It must be the first art competition she hasn't won."

"Yes, it was... I'm going to volunteer for Sea Watch as well," Antonia added. Mum was right. Sophie must have acted strangely because she'd been surprised. "Can I go to the beach with Sophie tomorrow afternoon? She said her dad will take us."

"Of course you can," said Mum. "Dad and I are going into town tomorrow afternoon so it'll save dragging you around with us. Now what would you like to eat?"

That evening Antonia found it hard to stop fidgeting. Her fingers kept straying to the dolphin necklace. What if the dolphins called her now? How would she get out of the house without Mum and Dad finding out? They'd never agree to her going down to the beach on her own. By bedtime Antonia was so jumpy she didn't think she could possibly sleep. Looking out of her bedroom window before drawing the curtains on the summer night Antonia saw the dolphins swimming in the bay. Bubbles, easily identifiable as the littlest, kept leaping out of the water. Antonia grinned, sure he was putting on a show just for her. The sight of the dolphins, *her* dolphins, reassured her. She didn't think Spirit would call her in the night, but if he did then she would find a way to answer his call. Antonia stopped worrying, climbed into bed and drifted off to sleep, to dream of dolphins.

Early the next morning Antonia's dad took her to Sandy Bay beach for her surfing lesson. Jessica insisted on going too.

"When can I learn to surf?" she asked as she watched Antonia pull on her wetsuit.

"When you can swim as well as Antonia," said Dad, ruffling Jessica's hair.

"You'll love learning to surf, it's great," said Antonia enthusiastically.

Jessica frowned.

"But that won't be for ages. Antonia's brilliant

at swimming. She swims like a dolphin."

Antonia jumped. What did Jessica mean?

"Naomi's sister says you're an ace swimmer," said Jessica wistfully.

Antonia laughed with relief. Naomi was Jessica's best friend and her sister was in Antonia's class.

"You'll soon be able to swim like me if you keep practising," she said as she fastened her wetsuit and picked up her board.

"Enjoy your lesson. See you later," said Dad.

"See you," said Antonia.

Under her wetsuit Antonia could feel the dolphin necklace pressing against her skin. What would her teacher say if the dolphins called her during her surfing lesson and she had to take off? The thought made her stomach flip. She wished she would get a call soon. All this waiting and wondering was making her head spin.

The surf was good. Antonia soon lost herself in the thrill of riding the waves. After her lesson she let Jessica sit on her board while she towed her along in the shallows. Jessica's eyes shone with excitement.

"I'm going to learn how to swim better quickly," she said.

"You do that," Antonia agreed. She loved surfing and wanted everyone else to love it too.

There were tuna sandwiches for lunch with cherry tomatoes, crisps and a glass of iced lemon. Antonia ate in the garden with Jessica.

"Can I come to the beach with you?" asked Jessica, through a mouthful of sandwich.

"Not today," said Antonia.

"Please? I don't want to go to the shops with Mum and Dad."

"Sorry, Jess," said Antonia. "But I'm going with Sophie and her dad."

"You're mean," said Jessica.

"No I'm not. You don't take me with you when you go round to Naomi's house."

"That's different," said Jessica. "Naomi's too small for you."

"And my friends are too big for you," chuckled Antonia. "Why don't you want to go to the shops? You'll have a great time. Mum will buy you some sweets if you're good."

"But I want to swim! And I want a necklace like yours. Can I try it on?"

"Erm, not now, Jess," Antonia scrambled to her feet. Was it her imagination or had the dolphin charm vibrated just then? Ignoring Jessica's cries for her to stay she hurried into the house, dumped her plate and glass in the kitchen then ran upstairs to her room. It was very quiet. Her silver necklace lay still. Antonia stood in a beam of sunlight spilling through the slanted window and tried not to feel disappointed. She pulled her swimming costume out of her drawer and put it on under her clothes. She might as well get ready to meet Sophie.

Antonia was bundling things into her bag when the dolphin charm juddered against her skin. She started, trembling with excitement as the dolphin charm started vibrating. The dolphins were calling. Antonia grabbed a towel, shoved it in her bag then raced downstairs.

"Bye, Mum, bye, Dad," she called.

"Not so fast," said Mum, blocking the front door. "Here, give this to Sophie's dad for ice cream." She thrust a note at Antonia. "And what time will you be back?"

"Teatime," said Antonia, hopping up and down. The dolphin necklace had started clicking. The noise grew louder as Antonia sidestepped her mother to pull open the front door.

"Ring me if you're going to be late," said Mum.

"I will." Antonia was amazed that her mother hadn't noticed the dolphin noises emitting from her necklace. The whistles and squeaks were ear-splitting. Antonia ran down her road towards the coastal path.

"Silver Dolphin," whistled her necklace. "Come to us."

"I'm on my way," Antonia whistled back.

As she reached the cove she wondered about getting into the sea: it was Saturday afternoon and even Gull Bay was busy. Would anyone try to stop her from swimming on her own? Antonia picked her way across the beach. Today there were no dolphins waiting for her, but the necklace was still clicking, urging her to get into the water. Antonia changed out of her clothes, put her bag on an empty patch of sand and took a deep breath. She was ready. She splashed into the sea, gasping at its coldness. The moment she was in deep enough to swim Antonia struck out in the water, breaststroke arms and dolphin legs. Her body moved like a real dolphin, her legs melding together like a tail. No one seemed to notice her as she swam towards the open sea, but in case anyone was watching Antonia dived down under the water just before she passed the orange safety buoy. Usually she could swim for fifteen strokes before needing to come up for air, but today her lungs felt stronger. Antonia stayed under the water as she swam further out to sea.

Chapter Four

She swam all the way to the mouth of the cove before surfacing. The sunlight was dazzling. Antonia screwed up her eyes and shook her head as droplets of water ran down her face and into her nose and mouth. Where were the dolphins? Were they in danger? She swam in a circle as her eyes searched for them. The swell was greater out here and Antonia had to kick hard to stop herself from drifting into the open water. When she swam out as the Silver Dolphin, her legs moved together as if they were joined like a tail. Antonia wished they would work like that when she was just swimming for fun.

"Silver Dolphin."

The call was so close it made Antonia jump. She spun round expecting to see Spirit behind her, but the sea was empty.

"Where are you?" she whistled back.

"Over here. Come and find me, Silver Dolphin."

Antonia hesitated, unsure whether to carry on. The water would be even rougher once she was out in the open sea. She had already broken her parents' rules by swimming alone and past the orange safety buoy. But what good was a Silver Dolphin who only stayed inshore? Convinced she was doing the right thing Antonia struck out for the open water. She had just swum clear of the cove when Spirit called again. His high-pitched whistling sounded from her left. Antonia changed direction, swimming faster as she headed towards the rocky coastline. Suddenly her skin felt tingly. It was a few moments before Antonia realised the tingling was coming from tiny vibrations in the water. Seconds later a shape swam past.

"Bubbles! Are you OK?" she exclaimed.

"You found us." He squeaked a laugh. "You passed your first test."

"I have to pass tests?" Antonia was surprised and felt a bit put out.

"Of course," said Bubbles. "You can only be our Silver Dolphin if you can do the job. There'd be no point otherwise."

"Well done, Silver Dolphin." Spirit and Star swam up with Dream trailing behind them. Spirit lifted his head out of the water, bobbing a half bow. "Your swimming is much stronger today."

"I can swim underwater for ages," said Antonia excitedly. "And I can feel vibrations in the water. I sensed Bubbles when he swam up behind me."

Spirit opened his mouth, smiling. "Now you are ready for your first task. It's a simple one to start with. Litter has gathered along the rocks; if left it will be washed into the sea where it becomes a danger to the marine life. I'd like you to clear it up."

"Of course."

Antonia smiled at Spirit, hoping he couldn't sense her disappointment. She knew litter was dangerous to turtles and seabirds, who often mistook plastic bags for food. But she'd hoped for something a little more exciting than litter-picking for her first job as a Silver Dolphin.

"Bubbles can swim with you and show you

where the litter has gathered. Any problems, just call me," said Spirit.

"Thank you," Antonia brightened immediately. It would be fun swimming with Bubbles.

The little dolphin obviously thought so too. He leapt from the water, his silver body curving gracefully as he flew through the air.

"Show off," clicked Dream.

"He's young. He's enthusiastic," said Spirit. "Come on. We're supposed to be meeting the rest of the pod. They'll wonder where we've got to."

Spirit flicked goodbye with his tail while Star lightly rubbed noses first with Bubbles and then gently with Antonia. She nearly fainted with excitement. Antonia still couldn't believe she was actually swimming and speaking with dolphins.

"Come on, Flipper Feet," called Bubbles.

Antonia snapped to attention and dived after

Bubbles. He was fast, reaching the rocky cliff face where it plunged into the sea long before she did. She raced after him, leaping in and out of the water, loving the way it felt as if she was flying.

"Now it's your turn to show off," said Bubbles. "I can't climb rocks or pick up litter."

He bobbed in the water, whistling encouragingly, as Antonia scrambled on to a cluster of rocks. The rocks were slimy with seaweed and she almost fell back into the sea. Her face fell when she saw the awful mess. There were crisp packets, drinks cans, polystyrene food cartons and a long tangle of fishing net. Bubbles became very subdued at the sight of the torn net.

"One of our pod got caught in an old net last year," he said.

"What happened? Was he hurt?" asked Antonia.

Bubbles shivered.

"It was a female and she drowned. We called for the Silver Dolphin, but we were way out at sea and it was too late by the time she arrived."

"Oh," Antonia's heart sank. She hadn't considered that she might fail at her job. The thought frightened her.

"That's why litter-picking is so important," said Bubbles.

Antonia carefully combed the rocks, not wanting to miss a scrap of rubbish. She found an old carrier bag, which she crammed most of the litter into. The rest she wrapped up tightly in the fishing net.

"Play time," said Bubbles. "Leave the rubbish bundles there and we'll collect them in a bit. Come and play Sprat."

"What's Sprat?" asked Antonia, lowering herself from the rocks into the water.

"It's a catching game," explained Bubbles. "You can be the sprat. I'll give you a three waves' head start."

It was fun chasing each other in the water. Bubbles kept leaping out of the sea to suddenly change direction. Antonia tried that too, but the move was harder than it looked and she ended up doing an enormous belly flop. It reminded her of a swimming game she played with Sophie called Sharks. Sophie! Antonia guiltily remembered she was supposed to be meeting up with her friend. What was the time now? Was she very late?

"Bubbles," called Antonia. "I have to go."

The little dolphin ignored her and swam further out to sea.

"Bubbles, I've got to go now." Antonia suddenly realised she was talking in her own language and called again, this time with clicks and whistles.

"Don't go." Bubbles twirled along the surface of the sea as if he were dancing on his tail. "Stay a bit longer and I'll teach you how to somersault."

Antonia knew it would be fun to stay with Bubbles, but it wasn't fair to let Sophie down.

"Next time."

Antonia swam back to the rocks to collect her bundles of litter. Towing them back to the shore was awkward. The bundles dragged in the water, slowing her down. Something transparent floated past her. Antonia reached out thinking it was a plastic bag then drew her hand back quickly.

"Jellyfish!" she squeaked.

Bubbles clicked a laugh.

"Jellyfish!" he exclaimed. "Sharks are scarier. They chase you. Jellyfish usually just float on past."

But Antonia was scared of jellyfish. She'd been

stung by one at low tide once when she'd been rock-pooling with her family. Her hand had swollen up like a balloon and it hurt for ages. She still had nightmares about it sometimes.

As they neared the mouth of the cove Bubbles slowed.

"I'll leave you now," he said. "The beach is packed and there are lots of swimmers in the water."

He dived under the water and surfaced a centimetre from her then gently rubbed his nose against hers.

"See you soon, Silver Dolphin."

"Yes," Antonia grinned. "Yes, you will."

She watched until Bubbles was out of sight before heading back to the beach. This time there would be no swimming under the water. She was carrying too much rubbish for that. Antonia hoped

that she wouldn't draw too much attention to herself by arriving on the beach looking like a floating dustbin!

Chapter Five

"There she is. I told you it was a simple mix-up. Hello, Antonia."

Antonia, who was cramming the broken fishing net into a litter bin, spun round, flushing guiltily. Sophie and her dad stood watching her.

"Sorry we're late. Sophie insisted she'd arranged to meet you at ours. We waited half an hour before I persuaded her she'd got it wrong.

I hope you weren't worried."

"It wasn't Sophie's fault." Antonia tried to apologise, but Mr Hastings waved it away.

"Of course it was Sophie's fault. She goes around with her head in the clouds. It's her artistic nature. Now how about I get you girls an ice cream while you find us a good spot on the beach?"

Sophie's dad didn't wait for an answer and strode off back up the lane towards the tiny wooden beach shop.

Sophie looked confused.

"You did say you'd come to mine, didn't you?" she said.

"I know. I'm really sorry."

"What happened?"

Antonia couldn't tell Sophie the truth, but she had to come up with a good excuse. Her friend was understandably upset.

"I've become a Sea Watch volunteer," she fibbed. "I was litter-picking on the beach and I forgot the time."

Sophie's voice came out in a high-pitched squeak. "You actually forgot me, your best friend, to do litter-picking?"

"Sophie, I didn't think..."

"Oh, just forget it," Sophie sniffed. "At least you're here now."

"I'm sorry. It won't happen again," promised Antonia.

She started to say more, but just then Mr Hastings came back grinning sheepishly.

"I forgot to ask what flavour," he said. "That makes me as bad as you, Sophie – two airheads together."

"And I forgot to give you this," said Antonia, pulling the money Mum had given her out of her bag.

"That's all right. It's my treat," said Mr Hastings.

The afternoon did not get any better. Sophie was being really quiet and anything Antonia did or said just seemed to irritate her. They were lying on their towels, drying in the sun after a dip in the sea, when suddenly Sophie sat up.

"Can I try your necklace on now?" she asked.

Antonia's heart skipped a beat and her hand flew up to cover the dolphin charm.

"Why now?" she asked, her words coming out in a rush.

"Why not? Unless you don't want me to."

"No, I mean, yes, of course you can." Antonia sat up. Her heart was beating very fast. The necklace felt like a part of her and she didn't want Sophie to try it on, but her friend was already reaching forward to take it.

"Careful," said Antonia. "Here, let me."

Her hand shook slightly as she undid the clasp and reluctantly handed the necklace to Sophie. What if Spirit called to her now? Would Sophie have a sudden urge to dive into the sea to answer him?

"A silver dolphin," Sophie mused. She turned the necklace over. "It's probably just sterling silver, isn't it? Dad bought some once to model with."

Antonia was surprised. Couldn't Sophie feel how soft the dolphin charm was? It couldn't be made from metal. To her it felt like a real dolphin. She watched anxiously as Sophie fixed the necklace around her neck.

"It's quite pretty, I suppose. We're going to a barbecue tonight. Can I wear it there?"

"No!" said Antonia, more forcefully than she meant to.

Surprise flickered across Sophie's face.

"Why not? I let you borrow my hair slide last week."

"We swapped hair slides. You wore mine and I wore yours."

"But we always lend each other stuff. Why won't you lend me your necklace? Don't you trust me?" said Sophie in a hurt voice.

Antonia was suddenly very anxious to get her necklace back.

"It's not that," she protested. "I've promised to lend it to Jessica because she wanted to come to the beach, but she had to go shopping with Mum and Dad instead."

"Oh, well another time then," said Sophie, handing back the necklace to Antonia.

"Another time," Antonia agreed, gratefully fastening it around her neck.

Sophie was very cool to Antonia for the rest of their time on the beach. Antonia was filled with a mixture of emotions. She wanted to make it up with her friend, but it was clear that Sophie was not going to be happy unless Antonia let her borrow the necklace soon. It was a relief when Mr Hastings said it was time to go.

The following day was Sunday and Antonia wished that Spirit would call, to justify her refusal to lend the necklace to Sophie. But to her disappointment the dolphin charm lay still. She wasn't needed. Antonia mooched about in the garden hoping for a glimpse of the dolphins, but the only thing she saw were speed boats and an aeroplane trailing a banner about the local aquarium.

On Monday morning Antonia was determined to be extra nice to Sophie at school. But Sophie was in a funny mood and hardly spoke on the way there. Antonia perched on Sophie's desk chattering away, asking her questions about the rest of the weekend, but all she got back were one-word answers. When Miss Brown finally arrived Antonia thankfully slid off the desk and went back to her own place. Miss Brown didn't let the girls sit together in class as she said they talked too much.

We always used to be chatting, thought Antonia sadly. She wondered if things would have been different if she'd lent Sophie her necklace.

Miss Brown had a new boy with her. He had dark curly hair and smiling eyes.

"This is Cai Pacific," she announced. "He's only here for six months so I hope you'll make him feel welcome. Cai is staying with his great-aunt, Claudia Neal; the lady from the Sea Watch charity."

Antonia looked at Cai with interest. It surprised

her to learn that Claudia had family. Somehow it made her seem more ordinary.

"Cai has lots of cousins who live in the West Indies," Miss Brown continued. "So if anyone wants an email friend then ask Cai."

He didn't seem to have any problems fitting in with the class. By lunchtime he was joking and laughing with everyone as if he'd known them for ages. The first lesson after lunch was DT. Miss Brown told 5B to work in pairs on their task to build a model Greek temple. Antonia assumed that she would pair with Sophie. But her friend had already agreed to work with Becky, as Lauren was away. Antonia was hurt. She and Sophie always worked together so how could she suddenly decide to pair with Becky, leaving Antonia on her own?

"Who'll make a three with Antonia?" Miss Brown asked the class.

Antonia forced herself to smile, determined not to show how embarrassed she was. Then Cai shouted out, "She can work with Toby and me."

Antonia's face flamed scarlet as she joined the boys. This was awful. She should be inviting the new boy to join her group, not the other way round. But she didn't stay embarrassed for long. Cai was easy to talk to and fun. His real home was in the city, but his parents had gone to Australia for six months to work so he'd been given a choice of going to boarding school or staying with Claudia.

"I hardly know my great-aunt, but I'd much rather stay with her than go to a boarding school," said Cai cheerfully. "Aunty Claudia runs Sea Watch from her house. It's so cool. I spent my first weekend here caring for an injured seal."

"That sounds fun. I might join," said Toby.

"Why don't you join Sea Watch too?" Cai urged Antonia. "You'd love it."

"I'm going to."

Antonia really wanted to be a member of Sea Watch and she also needed to speak to Claudia privately. Antonia felt sure that Claudia could answer some of the questions buzzing in her head.

"Why not join today?" said Cai. "Come home with me and I'll introduce you to Aunty Claudia."

Antonia glanced over at Sophie. They usually walked home together. How would Sophie feel about her going to Sea Watch after school with Cai? She was about to turn Cai's offer down when Sophie looked up. The two girls stared at each other, but before Antonia could smile Becky nudged Sophie and whispered something. Sophie snorted with laughter then Becky hissed, "Geek."

Antonia's face burned with angry humiliation.

What was Sophie playing at? Couldn't she see how spiteful she was being? At once she turned to Cai.

"Thanks, Cai. That'd be great."

Cai grinned.

"Wicked," he said. "I can't wait to show you the seal. We've called him Splash."

Chapter Six

At the end of school, Antonia nipped along to the office to ask her mum if she could go straight to Sea Watch.

"As long as you're home by five thirty," said Mum. "Don't forget you've got swimming club tonight so we're having an early tea."

"Thanks, Mum," said Antonia, scooting backwards out of the office and accidentally

bumping into Becky, who was walking down the corridor with Sophie.

"Ouch! Watch where you're going, clumsy," said Becky, deliberately throwing her bag in the air so the contents spilt across the corridor. "Now look what you made me do. Well, don't just stand there, geek. Pick it up."

"Get lost," said Antonia.

"Is everything all right, girls?" Mrs Lee popped her head over the office counter to see what all the noise was about.

"Sort of." Becky's mouth turned down. "Antonia bumped into me and made me drop my bag."

"Antonia, you really must be more careful," Mrs Lee scolded her. "Say sorry and help Becky pick her things up."

Antonia glared at Becky. "It wasn't my fault you dropped your bag."

"It was, wasn't it, Sophie?" said Becky.

Sophie went pink and said nothing.

"Antonia," said Mrs Lee, a note of warning in her voice.

"I'm sorry," snapped Antonia.

Furiously she picked up Becky's things. She didn't know what had got into Sophie, keeping quiet like that, but if that was the way she wanted to play it, fine. She'd not bother to stick up for her the next time she needed help. Antonia left school feeling angry, but she didn't stay cross for long. Cai was good company; chattering nonstop about Splash and how greedy the seal was for fish. He was so funny, Antonia was laughing out loud by the time they arrived at Sea Watch.

The charity was run from a big wooden shed in Claudia's large garden that sloped down to the beach. The shed stood right at the bottom with a

low fence separating it from the sand. Sea Watch also owned a rescue boat, which was pulled up on the beach. When they arrived Claudia was checking on a seagull with a broken wing. She was pleased that Cai had enjoyed his first day at school and she seemed even more pleased to see Antonia.

"I remember you. You're the girl whose poster won the competition."

Antonia's heart raced. There were so many questions she wanted to ask Claudia, but not in front of Cai. She hoped she would get a chance to speak privately with her. Claudia put the seagull back in its cage and moved on to a chough, a type of seabird. She spoke gently and the bird didn't struggle when she lifted it up.

"It's as if animals know she's helping them to get better," Cai whispered.

Antonia thought so too. There was something

special about the way the chough watched Claudia and the soft noises it made to her. It sounded as if Claudia and the chough were talking to each other.

Antonia helped Cai to feed Splash and fell totally in love with the seal. His liquid brown eyes reminded her of a friendly Labrador. He was funny too, nudging her hand with his whiskery nose if she wasn't quick enough to feed him another fish.

"Claudia says he can go back to the sea soon," sighed Cai. "It's where he belongs, but I'm going to miss him."

There were so many jobs to do – feeding animals, cleaning out their enclosures and tidying up – that the time flew.

"I've got to go soon," said Antonia reluctantly. "I've got swimming tonight and I said I'd be home early."

Cai said he was heading back too. "I'm

going up to the house for something to eat. I'm starving."

He said goodbye to Claudia, but Antonia hung back meaning to have a private word with her. She was wondering how to start when two girls arrived wanting to join Sea Watch. Antonia recognised them as Eleanor Jacobs and Karen Holmes who were in Year Six. Claudia gave the girls a warm welcome and offered them a guided tour. Antonia didn't have time to wait for her to finish and tried not to feel disappointed as she walked home. There would be plenty more opportunities to talk to Claudia now she was an official Sea Watch volunteer. Helping out at Sea Watch had been brilliant fun. Antonia thought she might quickly call in on Sophie on the way home, but then she changed her mind. What if Becky had gone round to play? Sighing heavily Antonia began the climb up Sandy Bay Road. She was halfway up when her skin began to tingle. Seconds later the dolphin charm began vibrating against her chest.

"Spirit," clicked Antonia, saying his name in dolphin language.

The dolphin charm vibrated more strongly and then began to whistle.

"Silver Dolphin. Come quickly."

Antonia raced back down the road towards Sandy Bay beach. A handful of people were still soaking up the sun, but most had packed up and gone home for tea. Antonia ran along the sand to the rocks where she discarded her bag and pulled off her shoes and socks. As if urging her to hurry the dolphin charm vibrated faster and the whistling became more shrill. Carefully Antonia clambered over the rocks until she was out of sight of the beach, then stepping across the rock pools she splashed into the sea. The moment the water reached her waist she thrust herself forward and swam. Her legs melded together as they kicked tail-like through the water. Her school dress flattened against her body so that she was perfectly streamlined. It was exhilarating, slicing through the water as if she was a real dolphin. Antonia couldn't help herself – in spite of the urgency she leapt out of the water, arching her body like Bubbles. It felt amazing, as if she was flying. Antonia continued to leap out of the sea as she raced towards the open water.

The waves were rougher out here. Antonia stopped leaping and concentrated on finding Spirit. She knew she was nearing the dolphins. She could sense them; her skin tingled with the vibrations in the water as Spirit and his family swam closer.

Chapter Seven

Seconds later Antonia saw them: Spirit first, followed by Star, with Dream and Bubbles vying to be third.

"Well done," clicked Spirit, swimming alongside Antonia. "You came quickly."

"You did very well," agreed Star, stroking her hair with a fin.

Antonia flushed with pleasure.

"How can I help?" she asked.

"There's a bird in distress, over there on the rocks." Spirit swung round so his nose was pointing at a jagged cluster of rocks sticking out of the water.

Wasting no time Antonia struck out towards them. The sea was even rougher here, slapping the rocks with angry fingers. Carefully Antonia swam towards a flattish rock with knobbly sides. She could feel the dolphins watching her as she reached out and clambered up the slippery barnacle-encrusted rock edge until she was able to pull herself on to its surface. She saw the bird immediately. A young seagull, its feathers still grey, staggering around on clumsy feet. A length of twine hung from its mouth and there was blood on its feathers.

"Peep!" it shrilled.

"Steady," whispered Antonia. "I'm here to help you."

She held out her hand. The seagull fixed her with beady eyes, but didn't move away. Slowly Antonia stepped closer until she could see the bird's pounding chest.

"Here, let me look."

Antonia stretched out her hand for the twine and followed it up to the seagull's beak. Gently she prised its beak open, gasping in horror at what she saw. A fish hook was lodged inside the bird's mouth in a tangle of twine and blood.

"Oh, you poor thing," Antonia spoke softly and the young bird cocked its head to one side as if it were listening to her.

"I'm going to get this out for you. It might hurt a little, but you'll feel much better once it's gone."

Slowly Antonia untangled the fishing line until she could see where it joined the hook. The bird's mouth was a mess and she used the hem of her school dress to dab away the blood. Then with gentle fingers she took hold of the shaft of the fish hook and, pushing it down, she unhooked it from the seagull's mouth. All the while the bird trembled, but didn't try to fly away.

Antonia wound the twine around the hook and put it in the pocket of her dress.

"Peep," said the bird. It opened and closed its beak then ruffling its feathers it flew up into the air.

"Peep," it called down to her.

"You're welcome," said Antonia.

She climbed back down the rock and splashed into the sea.

"Thank you," said Spirit. "It would have died if you hadn't rescued it."

Antonia felt elated. She loved being a Silver Dolphin. She didn't know why she'd been chosen for the role, but she was extremely glad she had.

"Can we play now?" asked Bubbles. "Please, Dad?"

Spirit opened his mouth in a smile.

"Yes, go and enjoy yourself."

"Bubbly!" clicked Bubbles. "Let's play Sprat. You're it."

He darted away before Antonia had a chance to catch him.

"Will you play too?" Antonia shyly asked Dream.

For a second Dream looked as if she might say yes, then Bubbles whizzed past them causing a mini tidal wave.

"Bubbles!" whistled Dream crossly. "No, thanks. I'm not playing with him," she added and swam after her parents.

Antonia was disappointed until Bubbles clicked, "Come on, Flipper Feet. You'll never catch me at

that speed," and forgetting Dream she raced after him.

Antonia loved playing Sprat with Bubbles. Her dolphin-like swimming skills were now so good that she almost believed she was a real dolphin. She raced through the water tagging Bubbles with her nose each time she caught him. After they'd played Sprat, Bubbles showed her a move he called the twister that involved leaping from the water and turning a circle on his tail. Antonia was hopeless at first and kept crashing down in a belly flop.

"If it's Splash you want to play then why didn't you say so?" clicked Bubbles, smacking the water with his tail to splash Antonia in the face.

"Eeeek!" she screamed, and splashed him back.

The water fight lasted until Antonia, gasping for breath, called a truce. It was getting late and although she could hardly bear to tear herself from the water she knew she had to go home. Mum would worry if she wasn't back by five thirty. Bubbles swam a little way with her, but he didn't want to get too close to the shore.

Antonia rubbed her nose against his, marvelling at how lucky she was.

"See you soon," she clicked.

"Bye, Silver Dolphin," Bubbles whistled back.

Bursting with happiness Antonia swam back to the shore. She wished she could share her amazing secret with someone. Sophie was good at keeping secrets, but Antonia wasn't sure she wanted to confide in her right now. Also she wasn't sure if she was allowed to tell anyone about being a Silver Dolphin. It was one of the things she somehow felt sure that Claudia would know the answer to.

I'll go to Sea Watch after school tomorrow, she decided, determined to get some answers soon.

As Antonia stepped out of the sea the water cascaded from her, leaving her clothes completely dry. As before, the only thing to show she'd been swimming was her damp hair. She stood for a moment wondering how that happened. It had to be a very special sort of magic.

Antonia ran most of the way home, arriving back at exactly five thirty. Mum was in the kitchen dishing up their tea.

"Hello, darling. Did you have a good time?"

"Fantastic," said Antonia, sliding into a seat at the table.

"Why's your hair wet?" asked Jessica. "Have you been swimming?"

Mum spun round from the cooker and looked at Antonia properly.

"Antonia, what have you been doing? You didn't go into the water without an adult, did you?"

"No," said Antonia, crossing her fingers under the table and hoping that Spirit counted as an adult.

"So how come your hair is wet?" asked Mum anxiously.

Antonia uncrossed her fingers and scrunched them into two fat balls.

"We had a water fight."

"What, you and Sophie?" said Jessica. "You two get all the fun."

"Not Sophie, someone else," said Antonia.

"Cai, the new boy?" said her mother, putting a steaming plate of lasagne down in front of her. "Well, I hope you're not going to get so involved with Cai and Sea Watch that you forget about Sophie. She's been a good friend to you, Antonia."

A good friend! That was a joke. Sophie hadn't wanted to work with her at school today and she'd let her take the blame for something she didn't do. If it hadn't been for Cai and her dolphin friends the day would have been horrible. At the thought of Sophie's unkindness Antonia's stomach flipped. What if she was still in a bad mood tomorrow and went off with Becky again? Antonia stared at the plate of lasagne. Suddenly she'd lost her appetite.

Chapter Eight

By midweek Antonia had never felt so miserable at school in her whole life. Lauren was still away and Becky stuck to Sophie like Velcro. Becky met them on their way to school, linking arms with Sophie so that Antonia was forced to trail behind alone. Thank goodness for Cai and Sea Watch to look forward to after school.

Frustratingly though, she still hadn't managed

to talk to Claudia. On Tuesday, when she went to Sea Watch there were so many volunteers there, all from Sandy Bay Primary, she hardly even saw her.

"You two know what you're doing," Claudia told Antonia and Cai when they arrived. "Please can you see to Splash first?"

The seal barked a welcome, greedily nudging Antonia's hand for fish. It was great fun playing with him. Antonia and Cai took him for a walk in the garden and he wriggled after them like a fat puppy. Afterwards they cleaned out his pen, fetched him fresh water, then took it in turns to feed him. Splash barked excitedly, trying to stick his whiskery face into the fish bucket.

Once again it was time to go home for tea all too soon. As Antonia left Sea Watch she tried not to feel disappointed that Claudia was still busy. She had so many questions to ask, Antonia was scared she'd forget them if she didn't speak to her soon.

"You never play with me any more," Jessica complained as Antonia came into the kitchen just in time for tea.

Antonia knew how it felt to be left out, so after she'd eaten she let Jessica drag her off to her bedroom to play with dolls.

"My doll's house people want to learn to swim," said Jess.

Antonia made them a swimming pool in an old ice-cream tub, and swimming floats by cutting pieces from her bath sponge. Jessica was so thrilled she kept the game going for ages. By bedtime Antonia was exhausted. She piled her clothes in a heap and crawled into bed.

"I hope I don't get a call tonight," she thought, sleepily closing her fingers over her dolphin charm.

But she knew no matter how tired she was if Spirit called then she would go to him.

On Wednesday, the last lesson before lunch was PE. Antonia changed quickly, tucking her silver dolphin charm inside her T-shirt so that Miss Brown wouldn't see it. There was no way Antonia was taking her necklace off. Apart from when Sophie tried it on at the beach, the necklace hadn't left Antonia's neck since she'd discovered she was a Silver Dolphin.

"Everyone ready?" said Miss Brown. "Good; walk down to the hall in pairs, please."

Antonia slunk to the back of the line. She was getting used to being the odd one out and wasn't going to ask Sophie to be her partner and give Becky the satisfaction of saying, "Sorry, Antonia, but Sophie's going with me."

The PE lesson was on jumping. *I wish I was doing this with Bubbles,* thought Antonia. She was far more graceful in the sea than on land and it was more fun leaping above the waves with her dolphin friend than charging around in the school hall.

"Antonia," Miss Brown's voice broke her concentration and Antonia landed awkwardly.

"I thought I asked you to remove all jewellery."

Antonia's hand flew to the dolphin charm that had worked itself out of her T-shirt. Blushing, she tucked it back inside.

"That's not what I meant. Take it off, please."

"But I can't..."

"I beg to differ," said Miss Brown coldly. "Remove that necklace right now."

"No, I mean, I have to..." Panic froze Antonia's brain and she was unable to string her words

together properly. She couldn't take the necklace off. She'd promised Spirit she would always answer his call. How would she hear that call if she wasn't wearing her necklace?

"Now, Antonia, or I will confiscate it for the rest of the day."

The class fell silent. Antonia could feel all eyes on her as Miss Brown held out her hand for the necklace. She knew she didn't have any option but to give it to her teacher. Miss Brown always carried out her threats and Antonia couldn't risk losing the necklace for a whole day. Hot tears scalded her eyes and she swallowed, forcing them back. There was no way she was going to cry in front of the class. Very reluctantly she removed the necklace and handed it to Miss Brown.

"Please, be careful with it," she squeaked as Miss Brown tucked it in her pocket. "It's valuable."

"If it's that valuable then don't bring it to school," said Miss Brown. "Carry on, 5B, the show's over."

Becky giggled then hurriedly covered it with a cough as Miss Brown glared at her.

"Valuable?" Becky whispered unkindly. "Tacky rubbish. That's what you said, didn't you, Soph?"

Sophie went scarlet and mumbled something.

Antonia felt like slapping Becky, but forced her hands to remain by her side. Let Becky and Sophie think what they liked. That was the least of her problems. What if Spirit called for her right now? True, it would be difficult finding a way to sneak out of school, but it wasn't impossible. Antonia remembered Bubbles telling her about the dolphin tangled in the fishing net that had died before the old Silver Dolphin had reached her. How could she live with herself if the same thing happened to her? And what if that dolphin was Bubbles?

Stop it. It wasn't helpful to think like that. PE only lasted for half an hour. It was unlikely that Spirit would call her in this short time so she must concentrate on getting through the lesson then ask for her necklace back.

Cai came towards her, jumping like a kangaroo.

"Don't worry, I'm sure you'll get it back as soon as PE's over," he said. Then, smiling encouragingly, he hopped away. Antonia began to feel a little better.

At lunchtime Antonia looked for Cai, but she couldn't find him anywhere.

"Where's Cai?" she called to Toby, who was kicking a ball around with his friends.

"Dunno," Toby panted.

The ball whizzed past Antonia's feet and Toby nearly tripped her up racing for it.

"Out of the way," he yelled.

Antonia moved quickly. She didn't want to annoy Toby. He'd been really nice about letting her partner up with him and Cai, and she needed some friends right now. She wandered around on her own until the bell went for the end of lunch. Then Cai appeared, running across the playground to join 5B as they filed inside.

"Where've you been?" Antonia asked.

"Nowhere special," said Cai vaguely.

Antonia was about to thank Cai for being nice in PE when she noticed Becky watching her. Becky whispered something to Sophie and the two girls sniggered. Then Becky puckered her lips and blew imaginary kisses in the air. "Ah, sweet," she said in a silly voice.

Quickly Antonia said, "Can I walk with you to Sea Watch this afternoon, Cai?"

"Sorry, I meant to say before, it's not on.

Claudia asked me to tell everyone that she's got to go to a meeting," said Cai. "So I'm going to Toby's after school."

Antonia felt utterly fed up. When would she ever get the answers to her questions?

Chapter Nine

The metal oil drum bobbed in the water as harmlessly as a log. Don't touch it," Antonia warned Spirit. "Let me check it isn't leaking first."

She swam round it, carefully checking for holes, and dived under the water to examine it below.

"It's fine," she said, pushing her long hair out of her eyes as she surfaced. "Luckily there's no damage."

"Is it poisonous?" asked Spirit.

"It might be," said Antonia. She looked back at the drum. "We did chemicals at school. That square with the big black cross inside means the drum contains something harmful. It might be slightly dangerous or much worse. It could be poison. Whatever it is, we can't leave it here. Let's get it ashore and then I can ask my dad or someone from Sea Watch to arrange for it to be taken away."

Antonia trod water, her legs moving together like a tail, while she thought about where best to land the drum.

"We'll take it ashore here at Gull Bay," she decided. "It's usually deserted at this time on a Sunday morning whereas Sandy Bay beach sometimes gets early-morning swimmers."

It was very early, even by Antonia's standards. She'd been woken by the shrill whistling of her dolphin charm and the movement of its tiny body vibrating against her neck.

Spirit!

She'd shot out of bed, thrown on her clothes and ran downstairs. In the kitchen she left a note for Mum and Dad telling them she was out helping at Sea Watch. Then sneaking out of the sleeping house she'd raced down the deserted path to Gull Bay. She'd known it was serious when she saw Spirit waiting for her at the cove's entrance. The dolphins preferred to keep out at sea.

"Where did it come from?" she asked, as she positioned herself next to Spirit along the drum's long edge.

"Who knows?" said Spirit wearily. "Things often fall off ships, even in good weather."

Together they pushed the drum towards the beach; Spirit with his nose, Antonia using her hands. She didn't like touching the drum much, knowing that its contents were harmful, and vowed to be extra careful getting it ashore, so that it didn't get punctured.

A gentle, incoming tide helped them push the drum along. Spirit swam as close to the beach as he dared without grounding himself.

"It's up to you now, Silver Dolphin," he clicked at last.

He nudged her encouragingly then swam back out to the open water. Responsibility weighed heavily on Antonia. She took a long, deep breath to remind herself that the difficult part was over.

"I can do this," she whispered in her human voice. "I can."

The drum bobbed away from her as the water grew shallower. She raced after it, her fingers scrabbling for its metal sides, and guided it towards the beach. When it was too shallow to swim she rose gracefully from the water and splashed through the frothy waves. It was amazing the way her legs felt joined together one minute then separate the next. Antonia concentrated on rolling the drum ashore. The moment the drum left the water it felt ten times heavier. Antonia could hear liquid sloshing around inside as she rolled it up the beach. It was hard work; the further she went the sand became drier and more powdery, so it dragged brake-like against the barrel. Breathing heavily Antonia pushed the drum all the way to the top of the beach. She stood for a moment to catch her breath, then with a final rush of energy upended the barrel to stop it from rolling away.

"There," she said, rubbing her hands in the sand to rid them of the metal feel that was setting her teeth on edge. "I did it."

All that was left was for her to tell an adult to arrange for the drum to be taken away. She was about to head home when she noticed that Spirit was hovering out at sea. Her necklace began to vibrate again. Squinting into the early morning sun Antonia could see he'd been joined by a smaller dolphin.

"Bubbles!" she squealed.

No way was she going home without saying hello to her dolphin friend. Antonia raced to the sea and threw herself into the water.

Bubbles was ecstatic to see her too.

"Flipper Feet, you're the best," he whistled, butting her with his nose.

Bubbles wanted to play and Antonia readily agreed to stay. Her parents would know where she was, well, sort of, and it wasn't as if she was doing anything special today. She dived after Bubbles, chasing him along the seabed, darting round clumps of seaweed until she tagged him on the tail and it was his turn to chase her. When they grew tired of that game Bubbles showed Antonia the twister again.

"You make it look so easy," Antonia complained.

"It is easy," clicked Bubbles. "Watch me again."

Antonia watched, marvelling at the effortless way Bubbles leapt out of the sea so he was standing on the water on his tail, then twisted round in a full circle. There was lots of laughing and splashing as Antonia practised the move until at last she could turn half a circle before her body collapsed and she crashed back into the water.

"Looking good, Silver Dolphin." Bubbles rolled in the water to show his approval.

"Good? It was brilliant! I'd like to see you try

walking on land," teased Antonia.

"But I don't need to come ashore," said Bubbles. "We dolphins keep to our own habitat."

It was true, thought Antonia. And maybe it would be better if some humans stuck to their own habitat too.

"Don't be sad," said Bubbles, playfully smacking her legs with his tail. "You're our friend."

"Why me though?" asked Antonia.

She had been to Sea Watch every day she was free, but still hadn't managed to have a private word with Claudia. Every time she'd sought her out the telephone rang or someone interrupted them. There was always so much to do at Sea Watch Antonia wondered how Claudia managed to find the time to sleep.

"I don't know," said Bubbles. "I'm just glad it is."

"Me too," Antonia rubbed her nose against Bubbles's. "Friends forever?" she asked.

"Forever friends, Silver Dolphin," Bubbles agreed.

The moment was broken when Antonia's tummy rumbled noisily.

"What's that?" said Bubbles, alarmed.

"My stomach," giggled Antonia. "I'll have to go soon. It's breakfast time."

"One last game of Sprat then," whistled Bubbles. "You're it."

He tagged her with his tail then, diving under the water, swam away. Antonia dived after him, kicking her legs with all her might to catch him up. Bubbles zig-zagged this way and that, making Antonia dizzy as she tried to keep up with him. Then he zoomed ahead and disappeared behind some rocks.

"Coming to get you," clicked Antonia, swimming the opposite way round the rocks to surprise him from behind.

She didn't notice the bright stain in the water drifting towards her until she was almost upon it. Antonia stared at the translucent cloud floating closer and suddenly she realised what it was. Horrified, she stopped swimming. Her heart was racing and although she wanted to scream, her throat constricted so that all that came out was a quiet squeak. "Jellyfish!"

Coasting ever closer was her worst nightmare. The largest swarm of jellyfish Antonia had ever seen.

Chapter Ten

Icy fingers of fear gripped Antonia. "Move!" shouted her brain, but her body refused to shift.

The jellyfish drifted closer. Any second now and they would be on her, brushing against her, setting her skin on fire with their stings.

"Silver Dolphin!"

Antonia's head jerked round in surprise. She had forgotten Bubbles, hiding behind the rocks.

"Swim out of their way. They won't chase after you."

Antonia stared at Bubbles. What was he saying? Panic had closed her mind and all she could hear was a high-pitched whistle.

Bubbles swam closer, nudging Antonia with his nose. His eyes beseeched her.

"Silver Dolphin," he whistled. "Swim with me."

Antonia looked past Bubbles, helplessly watching as the jellyfish came closer. What would it feel like to be stung by so many of them? What if they got tangled in her hair and stung her face? Antonia's heart raced, but she was still too scared to move.

"Silver Dolphin," clicked Bubbles.

He butted her in the back, pushing her clear of the jellyfish swarm until Antonia snapped out of her trance and began to swim. Blindly she splashed through the water not caring where she was going, so long as it was away from the jellyfish.

"Silver Dolphin, watch out!"

Glancing up, Antonia saw a lone jellyfish drifting towards her. She swerved left, almost crashing into Bubbles.

"Steady," he clicked.

Antonia kept going and Bubbles swam alongside her until at last he squeaked, "You're safe now. You can stop swimming."

Antonia shook her head. She wouldn't feel safe until she was out of the water. She swam on towards the beach.

"Stop," whistled Bubbles. "Silver Dolphin, come back."

"I can't," clicked Antonia, finding her dolphin voice again.

The water was getting shallower. Soon she could stand on the seabed. She gave up swimming and waded to the shore. Frothy waves broke on the beach and were sucked back into the sea. Antonia splashed through them, gritty grains of sand battering her legs. Suddenly something wet and slimy wrapped around her ankle. She screamed, imagining a jellyfish stuck to her skin.

Wildly she kicked her foot, but it was only seaweed. It plopped back into the sea and Antonia splashed out of the water and raced across the sand. She didn't stop running until she was off the beach. Looking back, she could see Bubbles out at sea swimming in distressed circles. Antonia turned away. She didn't want to leave him like this, but there was no way she was going back into the water. Not today.

By the time Antonia reached her house she had calmed down and was feeling slightly embarrassed. What must Bubbles be thinking? She hadn't even thanked him for saving her. If she'd stayed calm she could have worked out how to avoid the jellyfish herself. But they are scary when you are allergic to them. Antonia remembered how painful her hand had been the time she had been accidentally stung. She hadn't been able to use it for a whole week. Antonia stood at her front door wondering if she ought to go and find Bubbles and explain to him what had happened. But she wasn't keen to go back into the sea just yet.

Quietly she let herself indoors. As she climbed the stairs she could hear someone in the bathroom. Antonia sneaked past and went to her room, then threw herself down on her unmade bed.

Her dolphin charm began to tremble. Soon it

was vibrating like mad, its tiny tail thrumming against her neck. Antonia sat up, her breath coming in shallow gasps. Surely Spirit didn't need her help again so soon? Antonia ignored the vibrations, but when the dolphin charm started to whistle she unhooked it and shoved it right to the bottom of her sock drawer. Then she sneaked downstairs and phoned Sea Watch, leaving a message on their answer phone about the oil drum at Gull Bay.

Antonia left her necklace in her sock drawer all day and after much agonising decided not to wear it when dressing for school on Monday morning.

"I'm not scared of going back in the water," she said out loud.

It just seemed pointless wearing the necklace to school. How would she get away if Spirit did call her? She thought of all the excuses she could give for slipping out, but none of them rang true. She couldn't even say she had a dental appointment because Mum worked in the office and would know she was lying, even if everyone else believed her.

Antonia walked to school with Sophie, but they didn't say much to each other. Antonia was surprised that Becky didn't meet up with them, until they arrived at school and found that Lauren was back. At once she was glad, hoping this would mean things could get back to normal between herself and Sophie. But it didn't. Becky and Lauren included Sophie in a three and the girls stood in a tight huddle in the playground, whispering together. When the bell rang for the start of school, Lauren, who was much bigger than Antonia, barged into her in the cloakroom.

"Let's have a look at your precious necklace then," she sneered.

"I'm not wearing it," Antonia replied.

"Oooh! Why's that then? Did it break?"

Ignoring the question, Antonia took her lunchbox and pencil case out of her bag before hanging it on her peg.

"Excuse me," she said to Lauren, as she made for the classroom.

"*Excuse me,*" mimicked Lauren. "Aw, poor little Toni's lost her necklace!"

Sophie said nothing, but Becky and Lauren both roared with laughter.

"Ignore them," said Cai, following Antonia into the classroom. "They're just jealous."

It was sensible advice, but it didn't make the day any easier. Becky and Lauren kept making nasty comments and laughing meanly. Antonia couldn't understand why Sophie was still hanging around with them. She didn't say anything and she looked about as unhappy as Antonia felt. By home time Antonia had had enough. She was first out of the classroom, determined to walk home alone. Cai ran after her.

"Aren't you coming to Sea Watch?" he asked.

"I can't tonight," Antonia lied.

"Too bad," said Cai. "Claudia thinks that Splash is almost fit enough to go back to the sea. It might be your last chance to see him."

"Sorry," said Antonia regretfully. She desperately wanted to go to Sea Watch with Cai, but couldn't face seeing Claudia. What if she noticed Antonia wasn't wearing her necklace? Would she also know that Antonia hadn't answered the dolphin call?

"You'll come with me tomorrow?" Cai persisted.

"Yes," said Antonia, unsure whether she would or not. "I'll see you then."

Chapter Eleven

Antonia didn't go to Sea Watch the following day, or the next, and the silver dolphin necklace stayed hidden in her drawer. Antonia felt guilty about not wearing it, but she'd finally admitted to herself that she was scared to go back into the water. She wished she could tell her mum and dad about the fright she'd had. Her parents often made her feel better when she was worried or scared. But how could she tell them about the jellyfish incident when she'd broken the golden rule of not swimming without an adult, way past the orange marker buoy?

Jessica noticed Antonia wasn't wearing her necklace. "Did you lose it?" she asked.

"No, Jess. I just don't feel like wearing it."

"Can I wear it then?" asked Jess. "I love dolphins. They're my favourite animal."

"Not right now," said Antonia, feeling guilty at the look of disappointment on Jessica's face. Why did things have to be so complicated? Antonia was beginning to wish she'd never won the Sea Watch competition. But then she wouldn't have become a Silver Dolphin and that would be awful. *Or would it?* Quickly Antonia pushed the thought away. She did still want to be a Silver Dolphin. She just needed a break from it right now.

Cai suspected she was avoiding Sea Watch and asked her about it at school.

"It's not me, is it?" he said, pulling a sad face.

"Of course not," said Antonia. "I've been too busy to go this week, that's all."

"How can you be too busy for Sea Watch? You love it there. I've seen the way you handle the animals. You're like Aunty Claudia with them."

"You're great with them too," said Antonia.

"Aunty Claudia's amazed at how quickly I've settled in. She thought I might find it difficult coming from the city. But I just love being by the sea and helping out with Sea Watch."

Finally, on Thursday, the morning after Antonia had missed Splash being returned to the sea, Cai arrived at school with a message for her.

"Aunty Claudia wants to see you," he said. "She

asked if you could go along to Sea Watch after school today."

Antonia suddenly felt hot and her stomach flipped upside down. Claudia had been strongly in her thoughts over the last few days. Sometimes she imagined she could hear Claudia's voice encouraging her to wear the necklace. Antonia had thought this was just guilt at letting Spirit down, but now she wondered if there was more to it. Had Claudia been trying to communicate with her in some way? But that was impossible, wasn't it? As Cai finished delivering his message, Antonia suddenly felt all her worries bubble to the surface.

"Why does Claudia want to see me?" she shouted. "I haven't done anything wrong!"

"Whoah!" Cai raised his hands. "Don't have a go at me. I'm just the messenger. And who said you'd done anything wrong?"

Antonia stared at Cai guiltily. He'd been a good friend to her over the last ten days. So why was she taking her troubles out on him?

"I'm sorry," she said. "I didn't mean to shout. Things haven't been easy for me."

"I know," said Cai simply. "Go and talk to someone about it: your parents or Aunty Claudia. And if you can't tell them, then you can always talk to me."

Antonia smiled. She wished she could share her secret with Cai. It would be a relief to tell somebody. But what would he say if she told him the truth about being a Silver Dolphin? He wouldn't laugh at her, but he'd probably think she was mad.

"Thanks," she said.

Morning lessons dragged endlessly on. Antonia sat doodling dolphins on her exercise book distractedly and got into trouble several times for not listening.

"I don't know what's wrong with you today," scolded Miss Brown. "I'd rather have the old Antonia back than this new distracted one. You're away with the fairies."

"Or dolphins," sniggered Becky, pointing at Antonia's exercise book.

"Oi, dolphin brain," whispered Lauren. "What's it like having the brains of a fish?"

"Dolphins are mammals not fish and they're very intelligent – unlike you," Antonia retorted.

"Lauren, Antonia, that's enough," snapped Miss Brown. "One more word from either of you and you'll both stay back at lunchtime."

Lauren shot Antonia a poisonous glare.

"I'll get you for that," she mouthed. "I'll show you who the smart one is."

By lunchtime Antonia still hadn't decided whether

or not to go and see Claudia after school. She was a little in awe of her and though Cai assured her that she wasn't in any trouble, he didn't know all the facts. Antonia ate her packed lunch quickly then went outside. She found a quiet spot on the field and began picking daisies out of the freshly cut grass.

Should she go to Sea Watch or not? How much did Claudia know about her being a Silver Dolphin? Would she help or would she be cross with her for not wearing the necklace? Suddenly a shadow fell over her. Antonia looked up to see who was blocking the light. It was Lauren and Becky. Neither of them looked too friendly so Antonia just continued piling daisies into a mound.

"Well," said Lauren, squatting down and sticking her face right in front of Antonia's, "you going to say hello or something?"

Antonia lowered her gaze so she didn't have to look at Lauren's small mean eyes.

"Hello," she said, pushing a long strand of blonde hair away from her face, "or something."

"Hear that, Becks?" sneered Lauren. "Miss Fish-for-Brains thinks she's a comedian now. Well, we can show you something funny, Miss. This is for calling me thick."

Lauren snatched up a handful of grass then pounced. Taken by surprise Antonia fell backwards faster than a skittle. Lauren began throwing grass cuttings in her hair and face.

"Stop it," said Antonia, struggling to get up. But it was no use. Becky had joined in now and it was two against one.

"Look at her squirm," jeered Lauren. "What's the matter, Antonia? Don't you find it funny?"

Antonia began to gag. There was grass

everywhere; in her hair, in her eyes and up her nose. She couldn't breath and she couldn't swallow. She rolled on to her side, tears streaming from her eyes as Becky and Lauren continued to throw grass all over her.

"STOP IT!"

Antonia was dimly aware that someone was yelling at the two girls. Footsteps pounded closer and at last Lauren, then Becky, got pulled away. Gratefully, coughing and spluttering, Antonia sat up.

Chapter Twelve

Sophie stood with hands on hips, her blue eyes blazing with anger.

"Leave her alone. If you EVER lay one finger on her again then I shall go straight to Mr Cordier."

"Ooh," said Lauren. "What's with you? We were only having a bit of fun."

"Fun?" shrieked Sophie. "And would you find it funny if you were the one on the ground?"

Lauren sneered. She opened her mouth to respond, but Becky got in first.

"Come on, Lauren, we don't have to listen to this," she said. "Let's leave these losers together."

She whispered something else and Lauren laughed. Heads bent and still giggling the two girls sauntered away.

"Are you all right?" asked Sophie, brushing grass cuttings from Antonia's back.

"Yes, thanks to you," said Antonia. "I thought I was going to choke."

Sophie kept brushing grass, unable to meet Antonia's eye.

"I'm sorry," she said eventually. "This was my fault. If I hadn't been so mean to you none of this would have happened. I guess I was jealous of you winning that poster competition. I thought I'd win and I was disappointed when I didn't."

"Your picture was miles better than mine," said Antonia.

"But it wasn't," said Sophie, "that was the point. The competition wasn't about art, it was about caring for the environment. You're much better at that sort of stuff than I am. You're a natural when it comes to wildlife."

"It was my fault too," said Antonia. "I didn't turn up when we were supposed to go to the beach together. I would have been so mad if you'd done that to me."

Sophie took a deep breath. "Friends?" she asked.

"Friends," said Antonia.

That afternoon was so much better. Antonia really did feel as if someone had taken a weight off her shoulders. In the art lesson Miss Brown let the class sit where they liked. Antonia sat with Sophie and was so busy chatting she didn't notice her ponytail trailing in the paint palette, giving her hair green streaks.

"Antonia Lee!" sighed Miss Brown, coming to stand beside her. "Your hair is now green. You'd better go and wash it out before you turn mine grey."

"Sorry, Miss," said Antonia, trying not to laugh.

She scooted down the corridor, narrowly avoiding a collision with Mr Cordier. Antonia slowed down. If Mum heard about it she'd be in double trouble!

Cai looked disappointed when at the end of the day Antonia made an excuse not to go to Sea Watch with him.

"What shall I tell Aunty Claudia?" he asked.

"Tell her you gave me the message and I said I

couldn't come tonight," said Antonia.

She picked up her bag and walked to the door where Sophie was waiting.

"Antonia..."

Antonia spun round and looked at Cai expectantly.

"Er, I... don't leave it too late," he said, and shouldering his own bag he walked quickly past them out of the door.

"What was all that about?" asked Sophie curiously.

"Nothing," said Antonia briskly. "He just wanted me to go to Sea Watch with him."

"I don't mind if you want to," said Sophie. "We don't have to always do the same things."

"No, it's fine," said Antonia. "I really don't want to go to Sea Watch right now."

Later that evening, as Antonia got ready for bed, she badly regretted her decision to not go and see Claudia. All it would have taken was a bit of courage. Sophie had shown lots of courage today. First by standing up to Becky and Lauren and then by apologising to Antonia and admitting that she'd been jealous of her.

That was different, Antonia told herself.

She shook her head and tried to ignore her thoughts. Antonia walked across her bedroom and stared out of the attic window overlooking the bay. The evening sun sparkled on the water so that it seemed saturated with tiny jewels. Seagulls mewed overhead and a salty breeze stole into her room. Movement caught Antonia's eye and she saw four shapes leaping across the water. She screwed up her eyes to reduce the dazzle from the setting sun. Dolphins. Two large and two small came flying across the bay. Antonia caught her breath. They looked so beautiful skimming across the tops of the waves. Beautiful yet vulnerable. As one, the dolphins dived under the water. Antonia remained at the window, her eyes searching for them to resurface, but the dolphins had gone. A sob caught in Antonia's throat. She was a failure. She had been chosen to help not just the dolphins, but all creatures living in the sea. But she'd let everyone down.

Do something about it, urged a voice in her head.

Antonia jumped. Had that thought been her own or not? She closed her eyes waiting to hear more, but, like the dolphins, there was nothing else there. Suddenly she made up her mind. Sophie had been brave and now it was her turn. She strode over to her chest of drawers and burying her hand

inside the jumble of socks she pulled out the silver dolphin necklace. The chain felt cold and hard in her hand. Antonia fingered the tiny silver charm. That felt cold too. Cold and lifeless.

"No!" she cried.

What was it Cai had said about not leaving it too late? He didn't know about the necklace, or Antonia being a Silver Dolphin, yet he had been so right. With trembling fingers she fastened the chain around her neck.

"Please," she whispered, cupping the dolphin in her hand as if by doing so she could give it life. "Please, give me one more chance."

Slowly she climbed into bed, but sleep eluded her. Antonia lay staring at the ceiling for what seemed like hours until finally she slept, the dolphin charm cradled in one hand.

Chapter Thirteen

Groggily Antonia rolled over. Her room was still in semi darkness. She blinked as her grey-green eyes struggled to focus on her alarm clock.

"Four fifteen," she groaned.

She lay in the half-light wondering what had woken her. Then suddenly she realised the necklace was beating a rhythm against her chest. Immediately she was properly awake and, resisting the urge to cheer, she leapt out of bed and hurriedly pulled on her clothes. Round her neck the dolphin charm continued to vibrate, then suddenly it began to whistle. Antonia's hand brushed against it as she pulled on her T-shirt. The charm felt soft and slippery, just like a real dolphin.

"I'm coming," she whispered. "Spirit, I hear your call."

As she crept downstairs she wondered if she should leave a note for her mum and dad. They wouldn't be awake this time in the morning; even Dad, who was a mechanic and often left early to open up his garage, didn't get up until six.

"Better to be safe than sorry," she whispered as she veered into the kitchen to leave a note on the table.

The note written, Antonia pulled on her trainers, then carefully undid the locks on the front door. At last she was outside. The sharp morning air on her face was better than a cold shower to wake her up. The whistling from her necklace grew shriller, urging her to hurry. Stumbling down the coastal path, the first rays of sun barely penetrating the trees, Antonia wished she'd brought a torch to light her way. When the path forked Antonia went right, opting for Gull Bay, as it was nearer and more secluded than Sandy Bay beach. She ran on until at last she arrived, panting and with sweat running down her face. Up until now Antonia hadn't thought about going into the water. She'd been so relieved that her charm was working and that she could still communicate with Spirit, it hadn't seemed important. Now, as she stood on the beach pulling off her trainers and socks she began to have second thoughts. What if there were more jellyfish waiting to get her?

"Don't be silly," Antonia scolded herself out loud. Jellyfish didn't lie in wait for people. This time she would keep her wits about her and if she saw anything dangerous she would move away from it quickly.

Antonia ran down to the water's edge and stared out at the sea. At the mouth of the cove three dolphins were waiting for her. Antonia blinked and counted again, two large, one small. Who was missing?

Antonia took a deep breath and ran into the water. The moment it reached her waist and her legs felt as if they were melding together, Antonia experienced a burst of panic. For a second she was tempted to turn and run back to the beach. But the dolphin charm urged her on. Forcing the panic to the very bottom of her stomach, Antonia moved forward. When the water reached her shoulders she swam; with breaststroke arms and dolphin legs she sliced through the water until she was within a tail's length of the dolphins.

Spirit swam up to her, his liquid eyes brimming with emotion.

"Silver Dolphin, you came back," he clicked.

Antonia felt herself blush. "I'm sorry. I didn't mean to let you down. I was scared. Bubbles saved me, but then I was afraid to go back in the water."

"I know," said Spirit kindly. "But you have come back, and now it's your turn to help Bubbles."

Antonia stared over Spirit's head and saw that it was Star and Dream who'd come with him. Star was anxiously bobbing in the water and even Dream had lost her usually bored expression.

"Bubbles," she gasped. "Where is he? What's happened to him?"

"He was playing not far from where you came

across the jellyfish swarm when he found an old fishing net," said Spirit.

Antonia's insides turned to ice. Fishing nets were Bubbles's worst nightmare. Immediately Antonia forgot her fears and struck out to save her dolphin friend.

"Wait! Silver Dolphin, come back," clicked Spirit.

But Antonia barely heard him. There was no time to lose. She had to get to Bubbles and rescue him from the fishing net. Like a torpedo, Antonia sped through the water.

"Let me save him. Please let me save him."

She chanted the words in time with her arms as they pulled her through the water. There was no sign of Bubbles above the sea's surface so Antonia dived down and swam along the seabed. Ahead she could see a dark shadow. Was it jellyfish?

Antonia's stomach dipped with fear, but she just altered her course and swam around it. There were no jellyfish; it was a bed of seaweed fronds waving gently in the current. Suddenly Antonia's skin began to tingle. It took her a second to recognise that the sensation was caused by vibrations in the water. As she swam on, the vibrations grew stronger. A vivid image flashed into her head: Bubbles bound by a fishing net, struggling for his life.

"Bubbles, I'm coming," she whistled shrilly.

The vibrations were so strong that Antonia knew she must be nearly there. She swam on, thoughts forming in her mind. Dolphins could stay underwater for up to an hour, but they normally came up for air every ten minutes. Antonia had no idea how long Bubbles had before he needed to breathe, but if he was underwater too long he

would drown. With a superhuman effort Antonia swam even faster. The sea swirled around her, bubbling and frothing like the contents of a witch's cauldron. She hardly dared to look, not wanting to see her favourite dolphin trussed and thrashing around in distress, but Antonia forced her eyes open until, gasping with shock, she stopped dead.

Chapter Fourteen

It was a few seconds before Bubbles noticed Antonia was there. He was busy guiding something, splashing about in the water and churning up a storm with his flippers and tail. Antonia stared in disbelief as Claudia appeared, swimming behind Bubbles, kicking and writhing in the water too. As soon as Bubbles saw Antonia he stopped swimming and his mouth opened in a huge smile.

"Silver Dolphin," he clicked. "You came back."

"But..." Antonia was too relieved and bewildered to speak. She continued to look from Bubbles to Claudia as if she couldn't remember where she knew them from.

Claudia was clutching the edge of a fishing net, tugging it for all she was worth. She seemed startled to see Antonia, then her face broke into a wide smile.

"You came," she simply said.

They stared at each other for a long moment and Antonia felt Claudia's relief as clearly as if she had voiced her thoughts.

"But what if I hadn't?" asked Antonia, her fingers creeping to the silver dolphin charm around her neck. "What if I hadn't been wearing my necklace?"

Claudia looked concerned. "I didn't know it had

got that bad!" she exclaimed. "You should have come and talked to me about it. I'm always here for you."

Bubbles nodded in agreement and Antonia suddenly realised that she and Claudia had been speaking together in dolphin language. So Claudia was a Silver Dolphin too!

"But..."

There were so many questions, Antonia didn't know where to start.

Reaching out, Claudia put her finger on Antonia's lips to silence her. "Later," she said gently. "You came and that's what matters. I can rely on you to answer the call, Silver Dolphin."

"I thought it was Bubbles." Antonia's voice cracked with emotion. "I thought he was tangled in a net."

"I found the net," said Bubbles proudly. "I

needed help to move it before any more animals got hurt."

He shuddered violently and Antonia reached out and stroked his nose. When Bubbles stopped shaking she turned her attention to the discarded fishing net. The sight of it made her recoil. The net was full of dead things – rotting crabs, fish and seabirds. Anger surged through her making her head sing.

"How can people be so careless," she cried.

"Often it's through ignorance," said Claudia. "People don't stop to realise the consequences of their actions. That's where you come in. As a Silver Dolphin it's your job to help put right the wrongs of our world. By taking this net back to shore and getting rid of it properly, many sea creatures' lives will be saved."

"How will we get it back to the shore?" asked

Antonia. "It's too heavy to tow that far."

"I didn't know if you would answer the dolphin's call, so I answered it too," said Claudia. I'm not as strong a swimmer as I used to be, so I sailed out here in the Sea Watch rescue boat. I've left Cai back at the house. He's asleep, but I've left him a note just in case he wakes up."

"Does he know about us?"

"No," said Claudia. "I told him a boat had capsized and lost its net, and the coastguard had called to ask if I would retrieve it."

The net was extremely heavy, but with Antonia and Claudia working together and Bubbles swimming ahead, whistling words of encouragement, they managed to bring it to the sea's surface. As they broke through the water Antonia gasped at the sun rising up from the horizon; it looked as if it too had just burst from the sea. The colours were

a spectacular blaze of pinks and reds that spread across the water and into the sky like flames.

Claudia scrambled into the boat to haul in the net, but Antonia stayed in the water, partly to stop Bubbles from getting tangled up, but mostly because she couldn't bear to leave him again. Antonia shuddered as Claudia freed the dead creatures caught in the rope's squares and returned their bodies to the sea. She watched in silence until something nudged her in the side, making her spin around in the water.

"Silver Dolphin," clicked Bubbles. "Thank you for coming back. I couldn't bear it if I lost you. You're my best friend."

Antonia swum closer to Bubbles and rubbed her nose against his silver one.

"I can't believe I almost blew it. I'd do anything for you, Bubbles, and your family and all the other sea creatures. I'm so happy. I'll always be your Silver Dolphin."

Bubbles leapt at her, nudging her in the chest and splashing water at her with his fins. Antonia laughed and splashed water back until Claudia called for them to stop, saying, "We really have to go."

Bubbles nuzzled Antonia on the cheek. "I'll follow you home."

"I'd like that," she answered, nuzzling him back.

With Claudia's help, Antonia scrambled into the boat. Water poured off her and she shook herself like a dog.

"Thanks!" laughed Claudia, as she restarted the engine. "Antonia, wrap yourself in that blanket. I don't want you catching a chill with that damp hair, even if your clothes are already dry."

Claudia winked as Antonia wrapped herself in the blanket and Antonia grinned back.

Claudia turned the boat for home. Bubbles swam alongside, leaping in and out of the water until they reached the stretch of beach that bordered Claudia's garden. Whistling his goodbyes he swam back out to sea. Claudia and Antonia paddled the boat ashore and then jumping out they dragged it higher up the beach. Claudia glanced at the lightening sky.

"There are a few things we need to sort out," she said. "Then I'll run you home in the car."

Chapter Fifteen

Claudia chivvied Antonia into her kitchen where she began to make hot chocolate. She poured some milk into the saucepan then pulled out a chair for Antonia to sit down.

"I have always loved the sea and felt some kind of special bond with its creatures. Many years ago when I first realised how badly people were polluting the sea I was desperate to put things right. That's when I discovered I was a Silver Dolphin. It has been hard and often dangerous, but the job is very rewarding. Regrettably it became too much for me: I'm not the swimmer I once was. I knew I must hand the role over to someone younger.

Silver Dolphins are very rare and I'd been searching for a new one for ages when I decided to set up Sea Watch. Conservation groups can work miracles, but I knew I still had to find a Silver Dolphin. Then I had a brainwave: the poster competition. It was a way of promoting Sea Watch and there was a small chance it might lead me to a Silver Dolphin. When the entries came in I was very excited. Unbelievably, I had found what I was looking for, Antonia Lee was a Silver Dolphin."

Claudia smiled and Antonia felt as if a warm current had suddenly passed through her.

"So, Antonia, welcome to the Silver Dolphins. I'm very happy to be handing over to you. You are a very special girl."

"Why me?" asked Antonia. "How could you tell from my poster that I was the one?"

Claudia stretched out her long fingers.

"Intuition," she said. "Call it a sixth sense if you like. Your picture was full of facts and information that showed you knew about the marine environment. But I could also *feel* that you cared. When you write or draw on a page, you leave something of yourself behind. An essence. I also guessed that you have a special birthday. You were born on the twenty-first of June."

"How did you know that?"

Claudia chuckled softly at Antonia's puzzled face.

"Ah!" she said. "I knew because we are two of

a kind. We were both born on the summer solstice, the longest day of the year. It makes us even more special."

"Your birthday is the twenty-first of June too?"

Antonia was about to ask how that made them both even more special, but Claudia smiled mysteriously, then said, "Is there anything else you need to know about being a Silver Dolphin?"

"Yes, heaps!" said Antonia. "How does it work? Is it magic, that lets me swim like a real dolphin? Do I have to wear my necklace for the magic to work?"

"The necklace is merely a receiver," said Claudia. "Think of it like a mobile phone. It's the way that Spirit communicates with you."

"So it *is* magic," said Antonia, wide-eyed with amazement.

"The world is a magical place. Science goes

some way to explain the mysteries of life, but we can't know everything. All humans have the ability to tune in to things around them, but only those with a truly open mind can hear what is being said. You are willing to believe that magical things can happen to you. Believing is a powerful force."

Antonia sipped her hot chocolate while she tried to make sense of what Claudia had said. At last she asked, "So by believing that I can swim and speak like a dolphin I make it happen?"

"Yes," said Claudia. "But only a few very special people truly believe."

Antonia sat in spellbound silence until Claudia glanced at her watch and said, "It's time to take you home. Cai will be up soon.

You know he'll always be a true friend to you, even when others aren't."

"How did you know...?" Antonia started to ask,

but Claudia was busy rummaging in a drawer for her car keys and didn't answer.

"Here they are," she said, holding them up. "I'll run you to the end of your road. I won't go any further in case the noise of the car wakes your parents. Come along."

Stifling a yawn, Antonia followed Claudia outside. The sun shone brightly, promising another hot day. Claudia stopped the car at the top of Antonia's road and Antonia whispered her goodbyes as she climbed out. She stood waving until Claudia's car was out of sight, then turning round she began to walk towards her house. The birds were singing loudly and suddenly Antonia wanted to sing with them. She ran up her drive, but instead of going straight indoors she went through the side gate and into the back garden. She stood on the lawn looking out at the bay, her long blonde hair lifting in the breeze. Suddenly four dolphins leapt into sight tumbling in and out of the water. The smallest turned a somersault then, leaping high, he stood on the sea's surface and went full circle on his tail.

"The twister!" exclaimed Antonia, delighted that Bubbles was putting on a show. Her hand closed protectively around her silver dolphin charm.

Always answer the call, said Spirit's voice in her head.

"I will," Antonia solemnly vowed.

She took one last look at her dolphins playing in the sea, then smiling to herself she crept indoors.

Silver Dolphins

OUT NOW!

A storm wrecks a cargo ship in Sandy Bay and looters are everywhere. The dolphins are in danger. But how can Antonia help them when the beach is closed? Can she keep her friends secret any longer?

HarperCollins *Children's Books*

Read on for a sneak preview...

Antonia woke with a start. She couldn't see a thing, her room was blacker than a witch's hat, but she had no difficulty hearing the storm raging outside. The wind shrieked and rain drummed on her window sounding like pebbles being thrown against the glass. Sleepily Antonia touched her silver dolphin charm, loving the way it felt as soft as a real dolphin. She wondered what the dolphins were doing now. She hoped they were safely out at sea, dozing. Dolphins didn't fall sleep like other animals, they had to keep half awake or they would drown. Antonia closed her eyes and was almost asleep when a loud crack woke her. Having lived all her life in their little house overlooking the sea Antonia was very familiar with that sound. It was a distress flare. Immediately she was out of bed and pulling up the blind to peer through the slanting window. Another crack rent the night air and this time Antonia saw a spiralling plume of red smoke away to her left over Sandy Bay. Hoping that the life-boat crew would rescue whoever was in danger Antonia crawled back to bed. She slept soundly until Jessica roared in and shook her awake.

"Get up," she cried excitedly. "We're on the news. Sandy Bay's on television!"

"Whaa..." mumbled Antonia, pulling the duvet over her head to blot out Jessica's shrill voice.

Jessica gripped the duvet and tugged it back. "There's this boat. The *Princess Romana,* it got grounded in the storm and lost its cargo. Millions of boxes. And it's all washing up on Sandy Bay beach. Hurry or you'll miss it."

Antonia followed Jessica downstairs and into the kitchen where Mum and Dad were watching the local news on television. A picture of Sandy Bay filled the screen and Antonia gasped at the site of so many crates littering the shore line.

"The Italian cargo ship, *Princess Romana*, suffered some damage when it grounded and there's been an oil spill," said the news reporter, sounding grave.

To be continued...

Silver Dolphins
by Summer Waters